# Saving
# Adam

ADAM J Smith 4 year old

# Saving Adam

by

L. Smith

ISBN: 1-55517-480-9
v.1

Published Bonneville Books

Distributed by:
925 North Main, Springville, UT 84663 • 801/489-4084

CFI Publishing and Distribution Since 1986

Cedar Fort, Incorporated
CFI Distribution • CFI Books • Council Press • Bonneville Books

Typeset by Virginia Reeder
Cover design by Adam Ford
Cover design © 2001 by Lyle Mortimer

Printed in the United States of America

# TABLE OF CONTENTS

# Preface

*Saving Adam* is the real story of a real boy,
seen through the eyes of a real mother.

# MIRACLES

The last time I saw Adam he was on his knees, praying. This was also the last time that Adam saw me. We each had witnessed a miracle. My miracle was that Adam was serving as a missionary in England. Adam's miracle was that I was dead.

Considering Adam's start in life, I am not certain which was the greater miracle, if one could be rated greater than the other. Adam looked at me with a questioning look. I knew what his question was, which was the reason I was there. I smiled at him and gently shook my head no, which answered his question. I knew that this would be the last time I could visit him. His life, or that portion of it I knew, flashed instantly through my mind. I recalled the very first time I saw Adam.

# THE BEGINNING

That Friday had started off like most of my days, getting my older children off to school and performing the maternal duties required by my younger children: feeding, burping, changing, washing faces and other various body parts, laundry, cooking, holding, consoling, admonishing, warning, threatening, cleaning house, doing dishes, *ad infinitum*. I loved it!

Then the telephone rang, an event that was sometimes a welcome diversion, but at other times an unwelcome annoyance. This call did not fall into either category. It was bewildering. The caller introduced herself as a social worker from the Division of Children's Services. In my mind I immediately dismissed the call as merely another "wrong number." The bewilderment came when I realized that the call really was for me. Why call me? How did they even come up with my name? I never learned the answer.

Without any preliminary discussion, the social worker simply asked if I could do the department, and her, an enormous favor, and told me that she would need an immediate answer. Before I could say a word, she began telling me what the favor was.

Her problem was a twelve-year-old boy who was retarded, illiterate, completely uneducated and uneducable, and totally unmanageable. He had never been to a regular school. He made faces at people, as well as weird, irritating noises. At the moment, the boy was in a foster home, but the foster parents were insisting that he be removed from their home that day. He could not even spend another night with them.

The caseworker informed me that the boy would be committed to a state institution on Monday morning, where he would spend the rest of his life. However, the state hospital was at least one-hundred miles away, and it was Friday afternoon. There was no place available for him to spend the weekend.

Now came the favor: could I, would I, take the boy for Friday night, Saturday and Sunday?

Many thoughts flashed through my mind. The boy was twelve years old, older than any of my children. He was retarded and unmanageable. Would he present any threat, or actual danger to my young children? How would they react? Could I handle this boy when others obviously had failed? Because my usual response to the needs of children had always been immediate, my answer to the caseworker was: "Yes."

It was as though the social worker had not even heard my answer. A touch of despair in her voice, she said that she knew I would have to discuss this matter with my husband. The question was how quickly I could do that and call her back. Then it was her turn to be bewildered. I told her that it was not necessary to talk it over with my husband. We had what most people, I am sure, would consider an unusual relationship.

If it was okay with me, it would be okay with him. I told the worker not to wait for a return call, but to bring the boy.

While I did not deem it necessary to discuss the matter with my husband, I did feel I should at least notify him. I called him at his work and informed him that when he arrived home we would have a twelve-year-old boy staying with us, a boy who was retarded, illiterate, had no education, made weird faces and rude noises, and had behavioral problems which were apparently totally uncontrollable. As though he had been taking lessons from me in brevity, he simply said, "Okay."

This did not mean, or even imply, that I had his permission. I had not sought his permission, so he could not grant it. His answer told me that this was my call. One word had told me that my judgment did not need to be questioned. (I never could have married a male chauvinist!)

## DECISIONS

This was not the first time I had made such a momentous decision without first consulting my husband. After nearly eight years of marriage, my husband and I had never been able to have children of our own, although I did have one miscarriage. We had tried unsuccessfully to adopt.

Finally, after several false hopes, we were given the opportunity to adopt a beautiful baby girl. She was the light of my life, but that light was like a small candle when compared to the giant beacon she was to my husband. He couldn't run to the corner store for milk without offering to take the baby with him, just to give me a break. A five minute trip to the corner— some break!

Just ten months later I was visiting a friend halfway across the country. For some reason, the baby started acting up, throwing a tantrum in the middle of the floor. At that very moment, my friend's husband walked in. He was the doctor who had arranged for us to adopt our daughter. Hearing the commotion my baby was creating, he laughingly suggested that I was ready for a second child. But I took him seriously, and said that I would welcome the opportunity. He told me he had just delivered a premature baby boy who was up for adoption. In those days, it was common—and perfectly legal—for doctors to help parents find babies to adopt. I did everything that was necessary to take custody of this new infant.

Later that night, in fact, at about 3:00 A.M., I called my husband.

When he answered the telephone, I calmly stated, "Congratulations! You're a father."

"I know that."

"No, you don't. I mean you're a new father."

"I know that."

"No, you don't. I mean you're a new father again. You have a son!"

"I didn't know that. Okay, but are there any details you want to fill in?"

"No. We'll talk later. But there is one complication; the baby has a lung problem, somehow related to his being premature. He has been admitted to Children's Hospital, and he probably will be there at least two weeks, if he survives. I refused to let this complication interfere with my decision. I've taken custody of the boy and he is in the hospital under our name. If he doesn't survive, we will be expected to bury our only son, perhaps without your ever having seen him alive. If he does survive, we'll be responsible for his medical expenses."

"Okay. How are you holding up? Can I do anything?"

"Just pray. I have, and I feel that everything will work out okay. I'll stay here until the baby can be released from the hospital, no matter how long it takes. Are you okay being on your own?"

"That's a loaded question. I'm getting along okay, but I'll get along a lot better when you come home with my son and daughter. How are your parents?"

"They think I'm nuts."

"You are. Hurry home. I love nuts."

My parents, my friends, and the doctor found it incredible that I had made all of the arrangements before even notifying my husband, and that I never asked for his consent. I never felt I had to, and he never expected it. I guess this was an example of the biblical admonition for a husband and wife to become one.

A few years later, I got a taste of my own medicine. My husband arrived home late one night after attending a meeting in a neighboring state. I was fast asleep when he quietly crawled into bed, trying not to awaken me. I was only half awake when he gave me a kiss, turned over, and said goodnight.

After several minutes of silence, he started the following conversation, a dialogue I'd never forget.

"Are you awake?"

"No. Go to sleep."

"Okay. Goodnight."

"Goodnight."

"Oh, by the way, tomorrow we're going to have a new son and daughter. Goodnight."

I sat bolt upright in bed. "What?! Are there any details you want to fill in?"

"No. Go to sleep. We'll talk in the morning."

"How can I sleep? We'll talk *now!*"

The next morning we took into our care a little girl of about two years and her brother, about fourteen months old. Both had suffered from neglect and abuse. The state had decided to take custody of the children and place them in foster care. The grandparents learned they could avoid such intervention by moving the children to a different jurisdiction. With the assistance of their church leaders and the consent of the parents, the grandparents decided to temporarily place the children with a family in another state until satisfactory arrangements could be made for the parents to care for the children. My husband agreed to take the babies into our home.

While our custody was to be temporary, it was made clear that temporary in this case might mean anything from a few weeks to a year or more. The children's family members were to have access to visit them at any time. During the first few months, their father stopped by once and their mother and paternal grandparents visited a few times. We never saw the father again.

Shortly thereafter, the grandmother died and the visits by the grandfather and the mother suddenly stopped. We kept the children for more than five years and finally applied to the court for adoption on the basis that they had been abandoned.

When the mother was served notice of our petition, she appeared in court to contest the adoptions. The court appointed an attorney to represent her since she had no means to hire one. After the history of the case had been presented to the court, the judge ruled that the children had been abandoned. He noted that the mother had not visited the children in several years and that her appearance at this time was only in response to the notice of the court action. Although the mother had objected to the adoptions, she also made it clear to the court that she had no means and no intention to take the children back and no plans to visit them. Accordingly, the court ruled that parental rights be terminated and the adoptions were finalized.

My decision to take Adam into our home was only one of the unilateral decisions made either by my husband or by me. However, such decisions were not a source of contention between us, but a source of bonding that brought us even closer together.

# *WE MEET*

That Friday afternoon I met Adam for the first time. The state car pulled up in front of our house. Two social workers climbed out, followed by a young, skinny boy with dark, wavy red hair and a face delightfully covered with freckles. He quickly started playing with the other children, as loud and giggly as any pre-teen. My heart reached out to him immediately.

I was quite taken aback. He was not at all like I expected. To all outward appearances, Adam seemed as normal as any child I had ever known in all my years as an elementary school teacher. What I saw was diametrically opposed to the mental image I had formed. I became convinced that a terrible mistake had been made—not by me, but by them. I thought they had brought the wrong boy!

While the children were playing, I had a chance

to talk to the social workers and get a little more background information on Adam. I learned that he had been abandoned when he was two years old. I don't know if he ever knew his father, or if he ever knew his mother, or which one had abandoned him first, but at the age of two, Adam was abandoned, totally and permanently. I suppose it's possible for some children, when abandoned at such an early age, to completely recover from such a trauma, but abandonment, over and over again, was to be the pattern of Adam's life. He would not be allowed to recover.

Over the next ten years, Adam was under the "protection" of the State—closely supervised protection, and was placed in a foster home. I don't know how loving and supportive his foster parents were, but they apparently were not "long-suffering", and Adam was returned to the loving arms of the State.

By the time he had turned twelve, Adam had been placed in eight foster homes and eight times returned to the State by foster parents who could not cope. To Adam, each return was only another abandonment, and most certainly was his fault. Adam learned that if he did anything that angered his foster parents, even if he had no idea what he had done wrong, he would soon be sent to a new set of parents. A call would be made, and the state car would come.

On one occasion the pattern was broken. Adam was adopted. At last he could have a permanent home, with permanent parents. I doubt, however, that Adam fully understood the difference between being adopted and being placed in another foster home. I also doubt that he felt any sense of permanence. Even the smallest amount of conflict must have put Adam on watch for the state car. Finally it came. Adam's adoptive parents also could not cope. The call was made and the state car arrived. Abandoned again.

The cycle started over: more foster homes, foster parents, phone calls, more arrivals of the state car, abandonment.

Once again the cycle was broken, and for the second time Adam was adopted. Surely by this time the social workers had had enough experience with him to match Adam with suitable adoptive parents. But it was all an illusion. Again the adoptive parents were unable to cope. A phone call was made, and the state car arrived. Abandoned.

Finally, Adam was sent to his last foster home. These foster parents were different from all the previous ones. They were young, energetic, well-educated. They seemed to have a genuine interest in Adam and in his progress, or his lack thereof. He would be the research subject for their graduate study. Knowing that they would never find a real feral child— a child raised totally apart from human society—they viewed Adam as the next best thing. They would intentionally keep him in that near-feral state in order to study his behavior. He was the perfect specimen for the social scientists' "forbidden experiment."

This couple would sit for hours, silent, staring, notebooks in hand, annotating Adam's reactions in response to the various situations they would create. He didn't react the way he was supposed to, but more like a mental patient might: he opened his eyes wide and stared, making weird and inappropriate faces and noises that were rude and obnoxious. He was totally out of control, beyond all but professional help. The phone call was made, the state car came. Abandoned.

But, this abandonment was different; it was accompanied by the abandonment of the State as well as all hope. A mental institution was to be Adam's final destination. At the age of twelve, Adam could not read or write, although he seemed to speak as well as any youngster. Though he could not add, multiply, divide or subtract, he could dress and feed himself. In many ways he seemed like a normal child. But his education had been sorely lacking. Because he had been confined to special education classes his whole life, his only skill was coloring pictures with crayons. With this background information, I met Adam—or more accurately, although I did not fully understand it at the time— Adam entered my life.

## THE WEEKEND

That evening our family sat down for dinner. Adam just seemed to blend in with the younger children. I think he fit in so well because, socially, he did not appear to be twelve years old. What amazed me was that he demonstrated no signs of retardation or any type of behavioral problems. He did, however, exhibit one sign of the abandoned child syndrome: a fear of not having enough to eat.

Adam loaded his plate until there wasn't room for another morsel. Everyone noticed this, but no one said anything. As Adam glanced around the table with a worried look on his face, he was the one who broke the silence: "Is there enough for seconds?" He had not yet taken a single bite.

On Saturday we went through our normal routine with Adam joining in. On Sunday we all attended church, had a big family dinner, and spent the evening together. Adam was a delightful child, and we had an enjoyable weekend together. But it was to be only one weekend. That frightening thought persistently plagued my mind, even though I tried not to dwell on it. I shuddered at the thought—and wondered how Adam would react if he were allowed to know what I knew—the nightmarish reality that this weekend had been his last taste of freedom, that for the rest of his life he would be caged.

I could see nothing about Adam that should warrant his being placed in an institution, relegated for life to coloring pictures. Yet I knew that this was his destination the next morning. There must have been something that I was missing. Surely the social workers, with ten years of experience with Adam, must know something that I had not been able to uncover in just a couple of short days.

On Monday, I awoke to a humid, blistering summer morning. Our clothing stuck to our backs and our legs stuck to the plastic seats at the breakfast table. But only one thought stuck in my mind, and I knew that when the state car arrived, and Adam climbed in, only one thought could possibly be stuck in his: betrayal. If he had a second thought, it would be abandonment.

What had he done to be forced out of *this* family? What would he think when he was taken to the state hospital? I was the one who had let him down at the very end, the one who had betrayed him. I was the one who had welcomed him into my own family and made him feel at home. I was the one who must have made the call for the state car.

So I made the call. I told the social workers that although I was not related to Adam, was not an approved foster parent, and I had no legal basis for keeping him, *I* had Adam. I told them to save their time and effort. They need not bother coming for Adam, because I wouldn't let him go.

I knew I had no rights in this matter. I only knew that I was right, and that all of the wrongs were on the side of the State. *I* was not the one who had classified Adam as retarded. *I* was not the one who had proclaimed that he was uneducable and sat by while his education was limited to coloring pictures. *I* was not the one who had placed him in weird situations, and perhaps even dangerous ones. *I* was not the one who had sat by and watched a boy for ten years, noted his lack of progress, blamed that lack of progress on the boy's own mental deficiencies, and then proved his deficiencies by citing his lack of progress.

I had been told that Adam could never learn to read or write, but the only proof was that he was twelve years old and could not read or write. I was told that Adam could not learn basic arithmetic, and their evidence was that he was twelve years old and could not add, subtract, multiply or divide.

But I *was* the one who saw potential in his eyes, on his face and in his smile. I *was* the one who would lie down in front of the state car if necessary to prevent Adam's leaving. I *was* the one who would go to the news media and show that in a choice between my home and a mental institution, the institution was preferred by the state as a suitable home for this boy. If there were to be a war, let them come! I was ready to do battle!

## *THE BATTLE BEGINS*

That Monday morning, I saw the state car arrive. I was very brave in my thoughts, but what could I really do? Well, I was a woman and a mother, so I would do what a woman and a mother would do: I would bare my fangs, arch my back, and try to look as fierce and menacing as possible. It would be a look that at the very least would show that I would not retreat, not back down, that if a fight were unavoidable, I would welcome it, even relish it! It would be a look that said I would win!

Whatever the caseworkers saw in my face, or in my demeanor, I don't know, but it worked. After a brief discussion, the workers agreed that Adam could stay. Oh, they tried to talk me out of keeping him. They reminded me at great length of the terrible burden I would be undertaking, reminding me that Adam was retarded and had absolutely no education. He had never been able to learn, could not learn now, and never would be able to learn, had behavioral problems that were insoluble, and would be an additional expense. The other children might not accept him, might resent him. He might even pose some danger to the younger children. He would require constant care, not only now, but for the rest of his life. The State was obviously better prepared and better equipped to handle this type of child than I was. (I guess this supposition was not based on their previous ten years of success.)

Part of our discussion was regarding the means by which Adam's staying could be accomplished. Since I was not an approved foster parent, how could the caseworkers justify their actions to their superiors? Their first suggestion was that they take Adam and keep him in the institution until I could be approved as a foster parent, but I rejected this immediately. There was no guarantee that I would ever be approved or how long that would take. If I were approved, I had no assurance that I would get Adam back. There was also no way to predict how much damage would be done to him in the time he was institutionalized. And how would I ever repair the damage that would be done to my relationship with Adam if he thought that I too had betrayed him, abandoned him?

So the decision was made: Adam, for the time being, would stay. If the war had not yet been won, at least I had won the first battle. I was not really certain that a state of war existed, but I had to assume that it did until a final peace treaty was signed. I quickly learned, however, that my next battle was not to be with the State at all, but with Adam.

# *A RAY OF LIGHT*

I found that it was not true that Adam could not learn. He had learned very well: he had learned that he was stupid, retarded, worthless, and that he could never learn anything. Adam believed that lesson with all his heart. He also learned not to try, but only to fail. Failure was a kind of success to Adam, because it was what was expected. He had also learned not to complain, to do without. He had almost learned not to cry. But that Monday evening I saw a ray of light, or, more important, perhaps for the first time *Adam* saw that ray of light.

As we sat at the dinner table, (where many great discoveries are made) it was obvious that Adam was pleased to still be there, pleased that he had not been sent away in the state car. One of my children then made a startling remark to him: "Well, Adam, one thing about this family is that once you are in it, you can't get out."

Adam's mouth dropped open and his eyes widened in disbelief.

The child continued: "It's true. I'm adopted."

Before Adam could respond, a second child spoke up; "I'm adopted, too." Then a third and a fourth. Adam could not believe it. He turned to me for affirmation, and I assured him that what he had heard was true. All four of those children were adopted.

Adam turned to the other children and asked, "What about you three and the baby? Are you adopted too?"

To which my birth-son answered, "Nah, we aren't adopted, but we can't get out either."

Adam put his fork down, his eyes still wide, and said: "You mean that no matter what I do, I can't leave?"

All of the children laughingly assured him that he was stuck with the lot of us. But Adam wasn't laughing.

There was absolute silence for several seconds, all eyes fixed on Adam. I began to worry. How would he react to this? All of a sudden, Adam stood up, raised his right fist in the air, and shouted at the top of his lungs. It was only one word, but it brought tears to my eyes.... "Yippee!"

## *GLIMPSES*

We learned very little about Adam's life from him directly. Apparently he had successfully blocked out most of his earlier experiences. Only once in a while did we catch a glimpse of the horrors he had endured, and each glimpse was accompanied by a shudder.

For example, we learned that Adam did not know what a bed was. He had no recollection of ever having slept in one. He told us that he usually slept on the floor, and in one home he slept on the kitchen table.

The mention of the kitchen table triggered another recollection from his past. Adam recalled that in one of his foster homes he was told that children were to be seen and not heard. His entire day was spent sitting at the kitchen table with his hands spread out in front of him, palms down. If he spoke, or moved from that position, in his own words, "I got whacked!"

I said before that Adam had learned to do without, and I guess that all of us have had to learn that to some degree. But another incident showed me how different Adam's concept of "doing without" was from mine.

One afternoon, after a family dinner, we loaded all the kids into our van and drove to our favorite ice cream parlor, a dairy farm on the outskirts of town. As soon as we parked, the children jumped from the van and ran to the window to place an order for their favorite treats. As I followed, I suddenly realized that Adam had not left the van. I went back and found him slouched on the seat, chin on his chest and said, "Adam, come on. Aren't you going to get your ice cream? You can choose whatever you like."

He looked up at me with tears in his eyes and said, "You mean I get some, too?"

Upon questioning him, I learned that he used to go to an ice cream parlor with his foster parents and their children, but he had to wait in the car. The ice cream treats were only for family members. The state provided money for necessities only.

I took Adam by the hand and literally dragged him to the order window, telling him again that he could have anything he wanted. He asked me what they had, since he couldn't read the menu. When I'd finished reading the list, why was I not surprised that he wanted one of everything?

It was at another family meal where I learned an additional facet of Adam's background, one which was almost staggering in its implications. During the normal course of the meal, Adam had somehow daubed a piece of food on his cheek. He didn't seem to notice it and so made no effort to wipe it off. Quite casually I told him he had a spot of something on his cheek. But rather than simply wiping if off, he hung his head in silence, chin on his chest.

This reaction took me completely by surprise. But before I could say anything else, I noticed the tears streaming down his face. What had I said? What had I done? Was this the petty type of thing that previously had brought the state car and led to another abandonment? Did Adam think that this was grounds for expulsion?

Perplexed, I looked to my husband for help, but the blank look on his face told me I would have to look elsewhere. I told Adam this was no big deal; nobody was mad at him, that he should just take his napkin and wipe his cheek. No answer. Chin on his chest. More tears.

After two or three further attempts to assure him that no one was angry at him, but with tears still running down his face, Adam finally responded. Naturally I assumed that he would just pick up his napkin and wipe his cheek. But as soon as he started to speak, I recognized that his tears were not from fear, but rather from sheer embarrassment. Without lifting his head, he quietly said: "I don't know where my cheek is."

My heart sank. Tears welled up in my own eyes. Why had I assumed that Adam had had any type of normal upbringing? Through the blur of tears, I saw much more clearly. No loving parents had ever held him on their laps and played children's games with him, or read him stories. No one had taught him his ABC's, or even the names of the parts of his body. He had never heard a nursery rhyme. He had never played childhood games with siblings or neighborhood friends. For most of his life, Adam simply had been ignored.

# *PREDATORS*


It was during one of those rare occasions when we were able to get Adam to open up about his past that we learned the answer to a question which had long bothered my husband and me—why his most recent foster parents had been so insistent that Adam leave their home that very day. Why couldn't he have stayed even one more night? Were the faces he made at them and the rude noises *that* obnoxious? It never made sense to us.

Adam told us how they would sit silently for hours staring at him, watching every move he made, writing secrets in their notebooks. He didn't know how he was supposed to act. It made him feel like a caged animal, so he reacted like a caged animal: he opened his eyes wide, stared back and made faces at his audience. The silence was maddening and he broke it with strange noises, the stranger the better. His "captors" were bewildered, and enraged.

Adam had our younger children laughing hysterically when he demonstrated the staring, the faces and the noises which had forced him from his last home. What impressed me was that Adam apparently knew what would happen to him for acting out in such a way, but he acted nevertheless.

Adam's explanation answered why he had been sent away, but not why the *urgency*. We put the children to bed, then pressed him gently for more information. With his head hanging down, he admitted there was more to the story. For the first time we saw anger in Adam's face. It was the angry wife who made the call after learning that her husband had repeatedly subjected Adam to the most unspeakable acts. At first Adam had no idea exactly what was happening to him. What he did know was that he had suffered excruciating pain, which was temporary, and humiliation, which was permanent.

He has never been able to forget this horrible chapter of his life. Unfortunately, and unfairly, the memory is usually much shorter for such sick sexual predators. Hopefully, a vengeful wife can help keep the memory alive for the perpetrator.

How could the state workers have placed a child into this type of environment?

Was their screening process so inadequate, or was the placement made in total disregard of their understanding of the situation? These questions would never be answered.

# ADAM'S KEY

On Tuesday morning, I enrolled Adam in our public school, but he was assigned to a special education class. He had no background for regular placement. He was back to coloring pictures with crayons. I continually badgered the educational system to provide more for him than coloring books, but without success.

I spoke with Adam's teacher a number of times to see if there were not something she could do to start Adam on the path to learning. But she said she had other students to consider and could not have different students on different levels. They all had to stay together.

She claimed to be locked into the course material provided by the school district, and would have to prepare a special plan for Adam and submit it to the superintendent's office for approval. However, even if her plan should be approved, she had no way to implement it. She simply could not take the time to work with Adam on a one-to-one basis.

She finally made it very clear that she could not continue to have these discussions with me. The situation was simply out of her control. I would have to take up the matter with the District Office.

It took several calls before I was able to speak to the superintendent of schools, and that turned out to be a waste of time. Before I could even tell him what was on my mind, I was told that I would have to speak to the assistant superintendent, who was responsible for special education. Again it took a number of calls before I could make direct contact. By this time the secretary and I were on a first-name basis.

When I was finally able to talk to the assistant superintendent, I could tell I was not getting through to him, so I pressed for a personal interview. Getting me out of his office was going to be a lot harder than hanging up the phone!

I showed up promptly for my appointment, which in itself was a real accomplishment. As any mother with small children can attest, promptness lies very close to the line of being miraculous.

When I entered the assistant superintendent's office, there was not a single file on his desk, not a scrap of paper. I thought of the old saying that a cluttered desk was the sign of a cluttered mind, and I wondered if the same reasoning applied to an empty desk.

He greeted me warmly, shook my hand and flashed a smile so wide that it could only be classified as a grin. We had never met before, but he treated me like an old friend he had not seen in years. Reading his demeanor as condescending, I tried to explain Adam's situation, but the A.S.'s grin never faded. I knew I was fighting a losing battle. How I wished there had been a stack of files on his desk. Even a dirty Kleenex would have offered some hope.

Our conversation went along the following lines:

"How can I be of help?"

"My son is in your special education class, and I want to see what can be done to get him out."

"We can't get him out. State law requires that he attend school."

"No, I don't want him out of school, I just want him out of that class."

"You don't need my permission to get him out of class. Just bring in a note from his doctor."

"No, I don't just want to take him out of class, I want to get him out of the special education class and into a program that will prepare him to transfer into a class with a normal curriculum."

"We don't have such a program."

"You don't have a program with a normal curriculum?"

"Of course we do. We don't have a program to prepare a student with special needs to move into a class with other students who do not have special needs."

"In other words, you don't have a program for children with special needs, a program designed to remove those special needs."

"Typically those special needs will remain with the child throughout his life."

"And what if a student in your program is not typical? What if that child can learn to read, to write, to do math, to think? I am convinced that Adam can be taught these things."

"It's very normal for parents to think that their child is more advanced, or more capable, than he really is."

"Are those parents always wrong?"

"Almost always."

"You say 'almost always,' but I take it that you mean 'always.'"

"There have been many studies that show that the needs of these special children are irreversible."

"How many studies have been done on Adam? As far as I can see, there has been only one, and that has been done by me. I have started to teach Adam to add, subtract, multiply and divide. He is learning the times tables. He is learning to read and write. I have proven that he can learn, but I have only proven it to myself. How can I prove it to you? And when I do, what will you do about it?"

His smile began to diminish. "We have all the reports from the Division of Children's Services," he replied. "What we have here is a twelve-year-old boy who has been unable to learn any basic educational skills. His behavior is uncontrollable. His actions and reactions are inappropriate. His loud noises and facial expressions are inappropriate. To treat him like a normal child who can learn like a normal child would also be inappropriate."

"Those reports show that Adam has not learned basic skills, but they don't show that he cannot learn," I countered. "They report his making loud noises and rude facial expressions, but they make no mention of the circumstances under which he did those things.

Have you ever heard such noises or seen such faces while he has been in this school? Those same reports claim that Adam's behavior is uncontrollable. Have you had any behavioral problems with him in this school? I can tell you that none of these problems has surfaced in my home—not one!"

"I haven't had the opportunity to visit Adam's class, so I obviously haven't witnessed any of these problems personally."

"Have you had any complaints from Adam's teacher about any behavioral problems?"

"I'm afraid that I don't have the time to keep track of every single student. The best advice I can give you is to return Adam to the custody of the state and forget about all this nonsense. While I admire your good intentions, I must point out that children like Adam are best handled by professionals who have the requisite training and experience."

"Are you telling me that you are *not* a professional and that you do *not* have the requisite training and experience, and that you are in charge of the district's program for special education? I find *that* inappropriate!"

"I find it inappropriate to continue this discussion," he shot back, now without a trace of a smile. "If you have any further questions or suggestions, you should address them to the superintendent or to the school board. Now if you will excuse me, I have another appointment."

As I left his office, I felt defeated, then enraged. This was only another example of the source behind Adam's problem—abandonment.

I had just had a door slammed in my face by a system that was designed to open doors. To my left I saw another closed door. This door had the title "Superintendent" engraved on its placard. I stormed past the secretary. The look on her face told me she had seen the look on my face and that it was not in her best interest to try to stop me as I burst into the superintendent's office. The look on *his* face told me that he wished he were out to lunch.

"I want to know why you and your people are determined to destroy the life of a young boy!"

"I have no idea what you are talking about. We are not trying to destroy anyone."

"You are absolutely right. You are not trying. You are destroying a life without even trying. That is exactly what I want you to do—try.

"My son is in one of your special education classes. He is being destroyed because no one will try to help him. He's locked in a mental prison and you have thrown away the key. When I try to have a key made, you change the lock."

"Exactly what is it you want me to do?"

"At this point, I want you to do what you are obviously best at—nothing. Just get out of my way. I'll teach him what your people say he cannot learn. I'll open that lock and free his mind. I'll be his key!

"All I want you to do is to approve a program which I will present and when my son completes that program, I want him moved into a class with a regular curriculum. I want him in school with kids his own age. I want him to be a high school graduate. I want him to have a life. And I want your approval within one week, because that's when the school board has its next meeting.

"If I don't have an approval from you by that time, I promise I will have at least fifty mothers at that meeting, along with members of the press, and a lawyer. The mothers will be screaming to have your job, and my lawyer will explain to the board why he is going to file a lawsuit against all of you! The press will do what they do best, which is to make you look even worse than you are.

"Thank you for your time. Have a nice day!"

Within the week I had my program approval from the superintendent's office and Adam was on his way—away from special education, away from the crayons and coloring books. Like Pinocchio, Adam was to have a chance to become a real boy.

# THE TRADE

After many months, it still had not been decided whether or not Adam could stay with my family permanently. I was informed that in order to keep Adam we would have to apply to become foster parents and be approved. If we were not approved, Adam would be removed from our home. Worse yet, even if we were approved, a decision would have to be made at that time whether it would be in the child's best interest to leave him in my home or to institutionalize him. When I told my husband about this, he quipped, "Well it's just a question of who has the better madhouse."

I approached the caseworkers with another idea: why couldn't my husband and I simply adopt Adam? The response was that Adam may not be a fit candidate for adoption. After all, he already had been adopted twice and both cases had ended in failure. I found it interesting that in every case of failure, the blame had been placed on the child, and not on the adoptive parents or the State.

Another strike against us was that we already had four adopted children. Normally, a family would not be approved for a second adoption, let alone for a fifth. In addition, our house was too small. The state required that an adopted child have a room to himself and that the house have a specified number of square feet per person. We would have four boys sharing one large bedroom, furnished with two sets of bunk beds. In other words, we were three bedrooms short of qualifying. According to the state standards, we would have to give up two of our boys, or three if we were to adopt Adam. Based on these standards, we could not qualify either as foster or adoptive parents. In fact, we couldn't even qualify as parents.

I began to see how fine a line there was between reality and insanity. All of a sudden, we were on the defensive. We could not satisfy the state requirements, yet in every case where those requirements had been met, the result was failure. Could it possibly be true that Adam might spend the rest of his life in a mental institution rather than a home because there was an adequate number of square feet in his cell?

Amid the frustration, the anxiety and all the red tape, we were nevertheless encouraged by the caseworkers to apply to become foster parents. If approved, we were told, at least the State would compensate us with a monthly stipend for Adam's support. In my mind, such an arrangement was a form of betrayal to Adam, for we harbored no motive for profit in keeping him. We were not looking for compensation at all, but there was a certain logic to this procedure. We believed that the longer we kept Adam in our family, the better our chances would be for approval of an adoption. I asked the social worker if there was not some way we could be approved as foster parents without receiving compensation. There was not. The situation was ridiculous.

"Look," I told the caseworker, "let's make an even trade. I don't want the money, and you don't want the boy. Keep the money and give me the boy!"

They would make no such deal, so we applied to become foster parents. By this time we had discovered that nearly everything we had been told by the social workers about Adam's abilities was wrong. Adam could learn, he could interact with family members, he made no loud, obnoxious noises or rude faces. He certainly did not pose any threat to the younger children. In fact, he was tender and loving toward them. He presented no discipline problems at all.

In light of these facts, and apparently against all odds, we were eventually approved as foster parents. Encouraged by this success, we applied for adoption.

After all, we reasoned, the final decision would be made by a judge, and not by the Division of Children's Services. But could we win a judge's approval without the Division's recommendation?

Yes!!!

The court recognized that Adam had been a victim all of his life, that the possibility of his being a victim in our family was extremely remote, but that the opposite may well be true should he be placed in an institution. While the Division of Children's Services had legal custody of Adam, that custody was not designed to be permanent, as it most likely would be should the child be placed in a state institution.

In determining the best interest of the child, the limited space in our house was overlooked. The court felt that a family with other children, especially other adopted children, offered Adam much better opportunities than a mental institution. In addition, there was another safeguard. The state always has the power to intervene in case of abuse, neglect or abandonment and may quickly resume its custodial care of the child.

Based on the record presented, the court found that Adam had made significant progress in the few months he had been in our family, greater progress than he had made in the previous ten years in the custody of the state. Without the appearance of any potential harm to the child, the custody of the state should be terminated and the adoption finalized. I never knew what the state's recommendation was, but regardless, the adoption was approved and Adam became an official member of our family. The State kept the money and we kept the boy.

# *MADHOUSE*

I thought everybody I knew was crazy for thinking that I was crazy. To add to people's impression of my insanity during this period, I gave birth to another child, a beautiful daughter. But, as boys will be boys, they expressed their juvenile opinions that the new baby was "only a girl."

Though I now was the mother of ten children, five of whom were adopted, I never confused the names of my children. (That only seems to come with age). However, trying to keep track of their ages was another question. For two months of the year, my third child was the same age as my second. Then for the next two months, my second child was the same age as my first, except my first was no longer the first. Adam had come into the family as my ninth child, but being the oldest, he had assumed the position of first, and all the others slipped down a notch. Now it was my fourth child who was the same age as my third for two months, and then the third was the same age as the second.

In addition, my first child, who was now second, still insisted that she was first. Then it seemed that everyone wanted to be a *first*. My third child, who, because of Adam, was now fourth, insisted that she was first in the sense that she was my first biological child. My second, who was now third, insisted that he was first because he was the first boy in the family. My fourth, who was now fifth, decided he rated a first because he was my first biological son.

To confuse matters even more, my husband had convinced my fifth child that he was Chinese on the rationale that every fifth child born in the world is Chinese. But when Adam came, fifth became sixth, so my fourth became Chinese upon becoming fifth. Complicating matters further, the children considered my youngest daughter Chinese because she was my fifth biological child. Then they decided that Adam was Chinese because he was my fifth adopted child.

I really went bananas when someone asked me how old my children were. I finally worked out a formula to answer that question, and I revised it every month to keep it current. As an example, when Adam was fourteen and someone asked me the ages of my children, I would reply, "From one to fourteen, except for two, seven, eight, and ten."

# BRIDGING THE CHASM

I had only about two years to bring Adam from a kindergarten level to a ninth grade level. Or more accurately, I had two years to teach him the basic skills mastered by many of the students entering the ninth grade, a task which did not seem nearly so formidable when worded this way.

Over the next two years I immersed Adam in a series of crash courses in all subjects, trying to bridge an eight-year gap. There were many times when that gap seemed like a gaping chasm with no way across. And there were times when I felt like jumping into that chasm out of sheer frustration. Thank goodness I had nine other children to help maintain my sanity.

I had my work cut out for me, but I guess I never consciously recognized how much work that would entail. Although he did have a learning disability,

Adam continued to make progress. I began teaching him the alphabet, the basics of reading, and then the basics of arithmetic.

When Adam came home from school one day, I sat him down at the dining-room table and explained to him what "times tables" were. I then wrote out the multiplication tables from one through three and told Adam he had to memorize them. When he said he couldn't, I asked him why not.

Adam explained that he couldn't learn anything. All of his teachers, his foster parents and the case-workers had assured him that he could not learn.

How could I possibly break through this barrier? I knew I had one powerful weapon, and I decided it was time to use it. I informed Adam that as soon as he had memorized those multiplication tables he could eat!

I left the room, leaving Adam alone to ponder his fate, to wonder if he would ever eat again. Oddly, his look of despair gave me a sense of hope: the concept of "can't" was losing to the concept of "eat." About twenty minutes later he came to the dinner table with the other children. He recited the multiplication tables from one through three, and ravenously filled his plate to overflowing. "Eat" had won!

# *FREEDOM*

By the time Adam was old enough to enter senior high school, I was finally successful in getting him transferred from special education, and he entered high school with his regular class.

It was his first experience in a real school setting, a fact which escaped everyone at first. I took him to school his first day and helped him get settled in. Later that day I was working in the kitchen when I heard someone open the front door and enter the house. I was startled at first, but then I thought my husband must have come home, and I called out to him.

"Hi."

"Hi, Mom," came the response.

"Adam," I said, surprised. "What are you doing home? Why aren't you in school? You're not supposed to leave the grounds during school hours. Are you okay?"

"I'm fine," he said. "My first couple of classes were great. I got to do more than just color pictures. The teacher in my last class said our next period was free and we could do anything we wanted, so I came home."

Adam still had to learn the school routine, but on this first day, he learned one of the greatest lessons of his life: he could make choices. He was free.

# SOARING

Adam began to participate in all of our normal family activities, including the Boy Scout program, along with his brothers. Progress was always difficult for him, but the "carrot-on-the-stick" always seemed to work. I worked with him on every merit badge, and I am certain that each one took more out of me than it did of him, but he persisted and continued to advance through the ranks. He had learned not to quit.

During this time, Adam became friends with one particular boy. They spent a lot of time together, but Adam was often upset that his friend couldn't play some of the same games that he could. For his final scouting project, Adam devised and built a type of board game which could be played by his friend who was blind. He proudly presented several additional copies of this game to the local organization for the blind. With this act of compassion and true friendship, Adam stepped forward as the first in his troop to achieve Scouting's highest rank. He was an Eagle!

## *EXCELLING*

Dancing had been a part of my life for as long as I could remember. I could instantly learn a new dance step by seeing it done only once. I had always been able to easily follow the lead of any partner who knew the steps.

I introduced Adam to dancing, and anyone watching would have thought we shared the same gene pool. He was amazing. He practiced with his sister and learned all the right moves. He would go to a dance and lose his inhibitions. He felt socially equal to everyone there. He would ask any girl to dance and she would accept. *All* of the girls loved to dance with Adam.

I believe that dancing allowed him to operate on the same physical, mental and emotional level simultaneously, enabling Adam to excel.

# COMMENCEMENT

High school was a strain on Adam, and probably even more of a strain on me. *He* might have given up any number of times, but *I* wouldn't, and I wouldn't let him give up, either. Although I never had to threaten it, I always liked to believe that Adam remembered that lesson of long ago: stop learning and you stop eating!

Adam ate his way through the next four years during which he accomplished many things. But never was I prouder than when I saw Adam marching down the aisle with his high school class, dressed in his cap and gown.

It was a very emotional experience for me, but the tears came later when Adam gave me a gift to commemorate his graduation. He handed me a small package and told me he was giving me something that he would never need again. Bewildered, I tore off the wrapping to find a box of crayons.

# *REFLECTIONS*

I was aware of the long road that Adam still had to travel, but I felt great satisfaction over the tremendous progress he had made in such a short time. Research has shown that children who have been abandoned and raised in the type of circumstances that Adam faced never quite fully recover. There is abundant evidence that the brain does not fully and completely develop in children who have lived in conditions where they are not loved, valued or taught, especially for an extended period of time.

Besides me, whoever could have guessed that Adam would ever be a high school graduate? Certainly not his previous teachers, not the school administrators, not the Division of Children's Services, not the social workers, and certainly not Adam. He will probably never fully realize how much he has enriched my life, for which I will always be grateful.

Not once did my husband or I ever regret my initial decision to make Adam a part of our family. However, my husband used to tease me, saying that I could never really sleep well after taking Adam in, because it was his turn, and I could never tell when he would strike!

# GOODBYES

Adam graduated from high school in June. He spent the next year and a half working at various jobs, including a stint on a pineapple plantation in Hawaii. Then he prepared himself to serve a mission for his church.

At age nineteen, Adam was called to serve for two years in England. He looked so tall and handsome in his suit when the family took him to the airport. As I waved goodbye to him, I reflected on the past few years; the triumphs and joys and the difficulties and struggles.

I felt so proud of Adam as he boarded that plane. Tears filled my eyes and flooded down my face. They were tears of great joy, of fulfillment, of satisfaction, but they were mixed with tears of great sadness. As I waved goodbye to Adam, I knew in my heart that I would never see him again. This was really goodbye.

As hard as I had fought for Adam, I had been fighting for myself. During the previous two years I had undergone radical surgery for breast cancer. I had endured many hours of chemotherapy, which made me so sick I had wanted to die. I had made two trips to Mexico to obtain treatments which were not available in the United States, all to no avail. The cancer had spread throughout my body. I lost my hair and had to wear a wig whenever I went out. Every movement was becoming a struggle, and the trip to the airport was as difficult for me physically as it was emotionally. I sensed at the time that I was about to become bedridden. I was steadily losing weight and I was becoming weaker. To go to the bathroom, to join my family for dinner, or to attend family gatherings, I had to be carried.

Near the end of the year, I said goodbye to the rest of my family. I was released from my pain and suffering as I passed from this mortal world. It was Christmas Eve.

*****

## ABANDONED AGAIN?

The next day, Christmas Day, I phoned from England to wish the family a Merry Christmas. Many tears were shed on both sides of the Atlantic as I was told that Mom had died. I would never see her again. Why had she abandoned me?

I asked whether I should come home to help with the family or stay in England and finish my mission. Dad encouraged me to stay; it was the best way to honor Mom and to show my gratitude for all she had given me during the short time we had together. We both knew it was what Mom would have wanted, but it would be my decision.

Had I known at the airport that it would be the last time I would see Mom, I never would have left.

But I was wrong. I had not seen Mom for the last time.

# MIRACLES

That Christmas night, I was on my knees praying. As I pleaded with God to know whether or not I should return home, I became aware of a light in my room. I opened my eyes and there before me stood Mom. She was smiling broadly, radiant. I am certain that she knew the question in my mind. She slowly shook her head no, and I had my answer. I would stay.

In a tidal wave of emotion, my mind was flooded with thoughts of what she had done for me, how different my life would have been had she not entered it and how different it will be without her in it. Then she faded from my view and I was left alone, but *not* abandoned.

I don't know if I actually heard her final words, or if they were communicated to me in some way that I do not understand; what I do know is that they were words beyond my ability to speak. I knew that I would see that her story would be told.

Her last thoughts, expressed to me powerfully, unmistakably, were such that I can never forget them.

"OH MY SON,

IF ONLY TIME COULD BE REVERSED,

AND I COULD FIND YOU FIRST!"